D0398287

George Brown, CLASS CLOWN

Super Burp!

For Ian, *my* class clown.–NK

For Mom, thank you!–AB

GROSSET & DUNLAP
Published by the Penguin Group
Penguin Group (USA) Inc., 375 Hudson Street, New York,
New York 10014, USA
Penguin Group (Canada), 90 Eglinton Avenue East, Suite 700,
Toronto, Ontario M4P 2Y3, Canada
(a division of Pearson Penguin Canada Inc.)
Penguin Books Ltd., 80 Strand, London WC2R 0RL, England
Penguin Group Ireland, 25 St. Stephen's Green, Dublin 2, Ireland
(a division of Penguin Books Ltd.)
Penguin Group (Australia), 250 Camberwell Road, Camberwell,
Victoria 3124, Australia
(a division of Pearson Australia Group Pty. Ltd.)
Penguin Books India Pvt. Ltd., 11 Community Centre, Panchsheel Park,
New Delhi—110 017, India
Penguin Group (NZ), 67 Apollo Drive, Rosedale,
North Shore 0632, New Zealand
(a division of Pearson New Zealand Ltd.)
Penguin Books (South Africa) (Pty.) Ltd., 24 Sturdee Avenue,
Rosebank, Johannesburg 2196, South Africa

Penguin Books Ltd., Registered Offices:
80 Strand, London WC2R 0RL, England

Text copyright © 2010 by Nancy Krulik. Illustrations copyright © 2010
Aaron Blecha. All rights reserved. Published by Grosset & Dunlap,
a division of Penguin Young Readers Group, 345 Hudson Street,
New York, New York 10014. GROSSET & DUNLAP is a trademark of
Penguin Group (USA) Inc. Printed in the U.S.A.

Library of Congress Control Number: 2009036675

ISBN 978-0-448-45367-5   10 9 8 7 6 5 4

George Brown, CLASS CLOWN

Super Burp!

by Nancy Krulik

illustrated by Aaron Blecha

Grosset & Dunlap

An Imprint of Penguin Group (USA) Inc.

Chapter 1

Yo George,
 Never thought I'd say this, but I think it stinks that you won't be going to our school anymore. Now I'll be the only one in class 4A telling jokes, and my jokes always sounded better next to yours.
 At least at your new school, you can be the funny guy.
 Your pal,
  Kadeem

George lay on his bed and stared at Kadeem's page in the **Good-bye, George** book the kids at his old school had made for him. All the fourth-graders had written something. But Kadeem's page was the one that made George the saddest and the maddest. Sad because now he had no friends to tell jokes to. And mad because **Kadeem made it sound like his jokes were funnier than George's**. And that wasn't true. **No way!**

George reread what Kevin, his best friend, had written. At least Kevin used to be George's best friend. **Could you stay best friends with someone far away?**

George,
I was just thinking about the time in third grade when you put the fake spider on Mrs. Derkman's chair in the cafeteria. I never heard anyone scream so loud. I laughed so hard, milk came out of my nose.
   Boy, will I miss you,
   Kevin
P.S. Here's a photo so you don't forget what I look like.

George started to laugh. No one was more afraid of bugs than mean **Mrs. Jerkman**. (That was what George had always called his strict third-grade teacher—at least behind her back.) Freaking her out was always fun.

George turned the page in his book. The next note was from Suzanne Lock.

George,

Good-bye.
Suzanne

Even seeing that cheered George up. Suzanne hadn't wanted to write anything. Her teacher had made her do it. Not that George blamed Suzanne. It wasn't like they'd ever been friends or anything.

But the note on the page next to Suzanne's was from one of George's really good friends.

Dear George,
I'm really going to miss you. You made me laugh—a lot. I think you are really brave. I'd be scared to move to a new town. But you don't seem scared at all. I know you will have a lot of friends in Beaver Brook.
Your friend,
Katie Kazoo
PS—Thanks for the way-cool nickname.

George thought Katie's last name, Carew, sounded like a kazoo. And **the nickname had stuck**.

Katie was a really good friend. And she was pretty smart. But she was wrong about George. He was scared to be living in a new town and starting in a new school today.

George had a lot of practice being the new kid. His dad was in the army and his family moved around a lot. But it was never easy. After spending two whole years in Cherrydale, he had almost started feeling like an "old" kid. Then— *BAM*—**here he was in Beaver Brook**.

"George! It's 0-800 hours. Gotta get a move on! Front and center!"

His dad's deep voice echoed through the halls of their new house. It was a lot bigger than their old house. Even with all their furniture, it felt empty. In fact, the long upstairs hallway would be great for skateboarding—**except his mom never let him skateboard in the house**.

George grabbed his backpack and headed downstairs. For a second, he thought about sliding down the banister. Then he stopped himself. That was something **the old George** would do. Now, besides being the new kid, he wanted to be a new George. And the new George didn't do dumb stuff like that, dumb stuff that got him into trouble.

The last time George slid down a banister was at his old school. He'd flipped over the side of the staircase and wound up with a black eye and a bloody nose. And not just a regular bloody nose. **A super-colossal bloody nose.** The kind that turns your nose into a blood fountain. The school nurse said she'd never seen anything like it. It had been sort of gross. But sort of cool, too.

"Got everything, honey?" George's mom asked as he reached the bottom of the stairs. "Pencils? Notebooks? Lunch?"

"Check, check, and check," George said.

"That shirt looks really nice," his mother told him.

"Thanks," George said. His new green T-shirt had a picture of a blob on the middle of it. It was really cool. **The perfect first day of school shirt.**

"Okay, soldier," his dad said. "Ready to march?"

"Yes, sir," George answered. He saluted his dad. His dad saluted back and then gave him a big bear hug.

"Then let's go," George's dad said.

As George headed to his new school, he thought about Cherrydale Elementary School. Not to brag, but everybody there liked him. He was famous for being the funny kid—the class clown. Of course, pranks also got him into more trouble than anyone. It seemed to George that he'd spent as much time in the principal's office as he had in class.

But that wasn't going to happen in Beaver Brook. **No more class clown!** George was turning over a new leaf. He was through with getting in trouble. He was going to act differently from now on. So differently, in fact, that **he'd decided to start school with a new last name**. His dad's last name was Brennan. And that was the last name George had used all his life. There was nothing wrong with that name. But from now on, George was using his mom's last name— Brown. **New name, new George.**

"George Brown," George murmured

quietly under his breath. "George Brown."

"What did you say?" his dad asked him.

"I was just trying out my new name," George explained.

"Oh," George's dad replied.

"You're okay about this, aren't you, Dad?" George asked his father.

"Sure." Only his dad didn't sound so sure. "I guess it'll just take a little getting used to. But I **understand wanting to change things up**. Look at me. I've traveled all over with the army. New people, new places. Lots of changes."

That was true. His dad's job was the reason the family was always moving. It was why George always seemed to be the new kid.

"But we're going to stay at this base for a while," George's dad continued. "At least I hope so. Your mom is really excited about opening her own store. I don't think she wants to pack up and move again."

"Yeah, I guess," George said. Having a dad in the army was cool. But having a mom who owned the Knit Wit—a shop that sold yarn, knitting needles, and beads—was, well . . . not so much.

George kept up with his dad's long strides, trying to ignore the nervous feeling in his stomach. His mom called it having **butterflies in your belly**. But that wasn't what it felt like. It was more like worms. **Big, long, slimy worms slithering around inside.**

They turned a corner. There it was. George stopped and stared at his new school. It was a redbrick building with a flagpole in front. Over the door it said **Edith B. Sugarman Elementary School**. Except for the name, it looked pretty much like all the other schools George had gone to.

"Edith B. Sugarman?" George
wondered. "Is that somebody famous?"

His dad shrugged. "Never heard of her.
But the name doesn't really matter. Your

new school has a fine reputation."

George didn't agree at all. **Names did matter.** A lot. And no one knew that better than George Brown.

Chapter 2

"Class, this is George Brown. George, we want to welcome you to class 401."

George stood there, looking at all the strange, new kids, while his teacher, Mrs. Kelly, introduced him. It was awful. The kids were all staring at him like he was a freak—**a two-headed ape** or something.

For a second, George considered tucking his hands under his armpits, and saying "Ook, ook, ook" like an ape.

Nobody did a better ape imitation than George.

But no. He was the new and improved George now. **There would be no ooking at school!**

"Who will volunteer to be George's buddy today?" Mrs. Kelly asked.

Right away, kids slid down in their seats, so Mrs. Kelly wouldn't pick them.

George wasn't surprised. No one ever wanted to be the new kid's buddy.

Finally, a girl with a long ponytail, who was wearing a yellow and green Little League jersey, raised her hand.

George was glad someone had finally volunteered. **He just kind of wished it hadn't been a girl.**

Mrs. Kelly nodded. "Thank you,

Julianna," she said. Then she smiled and turned to George. "Why don't you sit at the empty desk in the third row?"

George walked to his assigned seat. He hated assigned seats. What if he didn't like the kids on either side of him? What if he became best friends with that short kid with curly hair and the mouth full of braces who was sitting in the fourth row? Or what if he got to be friends with the kid in the blue shirt in the second row? He was wearing the kind of sneakers that turned into skates when you popped the wheels out. **A kid with shoes like that had to be cool.**

Of course, that wasn't a problem right now—George didn't have any friends. **The new kid never did.**

"Okay, class, take out your science notebooks," Mrs. Kelly said. Then she turned to George. "Yesterday we were talking about the first moon landing."

George smiled for the first time that day. **The moon landing.** They'd already studied that back in his old school.

George's old fourth-grade teacher, Mr. Guthrie, had made learning about space really awesome. He dressed like an astronaut and made the classroom look like NASA's Mission Control Center.

Mrs. Kelly wore her glasses on a chain around her neck and had a piece of tissue tucked in her sleeve. And the only decorations on the classroom walls were a poster that said READ and a chart showing how all the letters of the alphabet looked in cursive.

"Now, who can tell me the name of the first man to step foot on the moon?" Mrs. Kelly asked.

Two hands shot up. One hand was George's. The other hand belonged to the kid with the cool sneakers.

Mrs. Kelly pointed to George.

"Neil Armstrong," he told her.

"Yes!" Mrs. Kelly said. **"Very good, George."** Mrs. Kelly smiled—the kind of smile where her gums showed.

George smiled back. Already he was being **the new, improved, raise-your-hand George**.

"The second man to walk on the moon was Buzz Aldrin," the kid with the cool sneakers called out.

Instead of telling him that he wasn't supposed to call out without raising his hand, Mrs. Kelly said, "That's right, Louie. Thank you for sharing such an interesting fact."

One of the other boys in the class said, **"What kind of name is Buzz?"**

George knew that Buzz was just the astronaut's nickname. He even knew that the guy's real name was Edwin. But he kept quiet. Yes, he wanted to be the new, improved, paying attention George. But no, he didn't want to show off or make the other kids think he was a **brainiac geek** or anything.

Instead, he kept quiet and copied down everything Mrs. Kelly said or wrote on the blackboard. **There sure were a lot of**

notes. After a while, George had written so much that he felt like his hand was going to fall off. He could almost picture his hand breaking away from his wrist, and then walking across the floor—like something out of a **horror movie**.

Finally, Mrs. Kelly put down her chalk.

"Okay, everyone, let's get ready for gym," she told the kids. "Mr. Trainer is absent today. So I'm taking over your class. And we're going to do something really fun." Again **Mrs. Kelly smiled her big, gummy smile**.

As the kids lined up, George thought that he was ready for some fun.

The short boy with curly hair and braces walked down the hall next to George. "**I guarantee this is not going to be fun**," he said in a low voice. "So you can stop smiling."

"Why? What's she gonna make us do?" George asked nervously.

"You'll see," the boy answered. "But trust me. **It's the worst**."

Chapter 3

George followed his new classmates into the school gym. The kids all had sickly looks on their faces. But Mrs. Kelly looked really excited.

"Okay, everyone choose your partners," Mrs. Kelly said.

George frowned. **No one ever picked the new kid as a partner.** He was going to have to do whatever the awful thing was all by himself.

"I'll be your partner," the girl named Julianna said to George. "Since I'm your buddy, it's kind of my job."

George looked around the room. Was this the kind of thing you did with a girl?

Or was it the kind of thing fourth-grade guys did together?

Then he saw everyone else had broken off into **boy-girl pairs**.

"Okay," he told Julianna.

Mrs. Kelly plugged her MP3 player into the speakers. Then she reached down and pulled something from her bag.

"Oh no!" The kid with the curly hair smacked his forehead. "Not the straw hat!"

"Alex, shhhh . . ." Julianna warned.

Mrs. Kelly was putting on a straw farmer's hat. It looked pretty dumb on her, especially since Mrs. Kelly was wearing big earrings and a necklace.

"Mrs. Kelly takes square dancing very seriously," Julianna whispered to George.

George's eyes opened wide. "Square dancing?"

Julianna nodded. "Mrs. Kelly loves folk dances."

George gulped. That Alex kid hadn't been kidding. This was **every fourth-grade boy's worst nightmare**.

"Now, class, it's been a while since we did traditional American square dancing," Mrs. Kelly said. "So I'll demonstrate a few of the steps again. I need a partner . . ." The teacher looked around the room. "George, how about you?"

George felt his eyes bug out.

"M-me?" he asked nervously. **"I've never actually square-danced before."**

"No problem!" Mrs. Kelly exclaimed. "This will be your first lesson."

Oh man. Like it wasn't bad enough being the new kid. Now George was going to be the new kid who dances with the teacher.

"Class, this is a do-si-do," Mrs. Kelly said, folding her arms in front of her.

George folded his arms, too.

"Now we walk around each other," Mrs. Kelly told George.

George followed whatever Mrs. Kelly did. As he circled around her, **the smelly, flowery perfume she was wearing made his nose itch**. So George wrinkled and crinkled his nose up and down as he danced.

George heard somebody laugh. It probably looked like he was making faces at his teacher. But he wasn't.

"Terrific!" Mrs. Kelly said. "Now we'll try the promenade. George, you take my hand and . . ."

George didn't hear a word Mrs. Kelly said after that. All he could think about was that he was holding his teacher's hand. And Mrs. Kelly's hand was all wet and sweaty. That was really bad because **George's palms were sweating, too**. That meant he was swapping sweat with his teacher.

One by one, Mrs. Kelly did the dance moves. They had strange names like sashay, do paso, and something that sounded like almond. And George had to do them all— with his teacher!

Finally, Mrs. Kelly sent him back to be Julianna's partner. Sure, he was still going to have to square-dance. But at least Julianna was a kid.

Mrs. Kelly turned on the music. Then she began **clapping her hands** and **stomping her foot**.

"Okay, swing your partner, 'round you go," Mrs. Kelly called out to the beat of the music. "Then everybody do-si-do."

Then Mrs. Kelly did something **really weird**. She started to yodel. "Yodelay-hee-hoo."

"Now promenade your partner home," Mrs. Kelly said. "Come on now, don't let her roam."

Huh? George had already forgotten what "promenade" meant.

But Julianna knew. She grabbed George's hands and started dragging him around the gym floor.

"Allemande left, and meet your friends," Mrs. Kelly called. "Then turn around and come back again."

Now George was totally confused. Was he supposed to turn to the left? Or was he supposed to turn all the way around?

Since George wasn't sure what to do, he did both. He spun around to the left, and then . . .

29

Thud. George tripped and landed right on his butt.

"Oomph!" George groaned.

Some kids started laughing.

Mrs. Kelly came over. "Are you all right?" she asked.

George looked down at his untied shoe. "Yeah," he said. "I just tripped over my shoelace."

George wished the kids would stop laughing. George didn't want Mrs. Kelly to think he'd been making fun of square dancing.

But Mrs. Kelly wasn't angry. In fact, she gave George **a big, gummy smile**. "It's okay," she assured him.

"Maybe I should just sit out and watch," George suggested hopefully. "So I don't mess things up for everyone else. **I could learn a lot by watching**."

"Don't be silly," Mrs. Kelly said. "Just tie your shoelace and get ready to do-si-do."

"Yes, Mrs. Kelly," George said. He stood up and got ready to do-si-do one more time.

A few moments later, the kids were dancing again. "Eee-hah!" Mrs. Kelly kept shouting and stomping her foot. "Swing your partner 'round and 'round. Don't let those feet leave the ground."

George tried his hardest not to fall again. **Boy, Edith B. Sugarman Elementary School was definitely a strange place.**

Chapter 4

It was amazing **how hungry** do-si-doing and allemanding could make a kid. **George was starving by lunchtime.**

His mom had packed a bag lunch, but he also had money for a snack. So he followed Julianna to the food line, and got dessert. All that was left was a block of Jell-O with whipped cream on top.

George carried his tray to where the kids in class 401 were sitting. They were talking and kidding around, just the way the kids at George's old school used to. The only difference was that nobody here was shouting, **"Hey, George, over here. I saved you a seat."**

Since all the boys were on one side of the long cafeteria table, George walked over and started to sit at the end next to Louie, the kid with the cool sneakers. But a boy with red hair and freckles pushed him aside.

"Sorry, **New Kid**," the kid with red hair said. "I always sit on Louie's left at lunch. Right, Louie?"

"Right, Mike," Louie told him.

"And I always get to sit on his right," a tall, skinny kid with brown hair said. "Right, Louie?"

Louie nodded. He turned to George.

"Why don't you go sit next to your buddy?" Louie pointed to where all the girls were sitting.

There was nothing else for George to do. He sat down next to Julianna.

Julianna was eating a **slice of cafeteria pizza**. It didn't look too bad. But the girl who sat down on his other side—George heard Julianna call her Sage—had a giant-sized plate of vegetables. Before taking a bite, **she sprinkled on a whole packet of pepper**.

"Hey, Louie, want to play killer ball at recess?" the kid with red hair asked.

"What's killer ball?" George asked.

"It's this amazing game Louie made up," Mike said.

"Cool!" George said, hoping someone would say, "We'll teach you how to play." But no one did.

As the kids talked about who was on which team for killer ball, George sat quietly drinking his milk and finishing the baloney sandwich his mom had made him. **George stared at his Jell-O.**

Ooh. That dessert looked so good. But

not to eat. What George really, really
wanted was to shove the whole block of
Jell-O into his mouth, chew, and then
slide the **chewed-up red slime** through
spaces between his teeth until it dribbled
down his chin.

George finished off the whipped cream, then balanced the Jell-O on his fork and was **all ready to cram it in**. But he stopped. George reminded himself that he was trying to stay out of trouble. So he dumped the Jell-O back on his plate and watched the girl next to him pour another packet of pepper onto her mountain of carrots.

George couldn't believe it. **What kind of kid liked pepper?**

Apparently, **Carrot Girl** was that kind of kid. She was already opening up a third packet of pepper when a kid returning a tray bumped her arm. Pepper flew onto George's tray.

"Ah-choo!"

The pepper made George sneeze. Two times. And the second sneeze was a big, wet one. George could feel two ropes of

snot hanging from his nose. Quickly, he
wiped his nose on his sleeve.

But it was too late. Louie had already
seen the whole thing. "How am I
supposed to eat when I have to look at
New Kid snot?" he asked.

George was about to say sorry, but he didn't get the chance. He sneezed again. **Two ropes of snot** flew out of his nose and shot across the table—**right onto Louie's tray**.

"Ooh, gross," the girls all said. But they were laughing. So was everybody else, except Louie. Sage was laughing so hard, she looked like she was going to choke on her carrots.

Teachers never liked when there was too much laughing in school. A few giggles were okay. But not this kind of laughing. George wished the kids would stop before the grown-ups heard them.

But the cafeteria lady had already seen the commotion. And she was on her way over to George's table.

Uh-oh. Cafeteria ladies hated him.

"What's the problem here?" the cafeteria lady asked.

"The problem is my tray," Louie said. "It's got New Kid snot all over it." Louie pointed to George. "He thinks that's funny."

George couldn't believe it! Louie was making it sound like George had snotted on his tray on purpose. **But he hadn't. He'd just sneezed.**

"That's disgusting," the cafeteria lady told George. "Today you can stay here with me during recess, so we can go over some of the cafeteria rules."

"But—" George started to explain. The cafeteria lady didn't stick around to listen.

As she walked away, George stared at Louie. "It was an accident. You know that!"

Louie smiled at him. "I was just trying to help."

"Huh?" George said. Since when was squealing on someone helping?

"Now you can find out everything there is to know about the cafeteria," Louie explained. Then he got up and headed toward the door. "Okay, guys. **Time for killer ball**."

George frowned as he watched Louie. "Next time, don't do me any favors."

Chapter 5

Walking home from school was really, really lonely. **"Just me, myself, and I,"** George said. There was no one else to talk to.

Later, when his mom asked how everything went, George said, "Okay." But his mom probably could tell it hadn't been the greatest day of his life because after dinner his parents took him out for **a special first-day-of-school treat**. They went to a place called **Ernie's Ice Cream Emporium**. It was the biggest ice cream parlor George had ever seen. It took up half the block!

Ernie's was a really cool place.
Outside, there were small, metal tables set up. Each had a cheery, red and white striped umbrella that was open even though it was nighttime and it wasn't raining. Inside, there were booths with bright red, leather benches.

"Can we sit outside?" George asked. "I want to be able to see the sky."

That wasn't the real reason. **The real reason was Louie.** When they had gotten out of the car, George had spotted him walking inside with a bunch of older guys.

"So, how'd it go?" his dad asked as they sat down at a table.

The last thing George wanted was a long talk about trying to "adjust." **He just wanted to enjoy his ice cream.** So he was glad that before he could answer, a girl in a black sweater and a red and white polka-dot skirt roller-skated up to the table. George smiled in spite of himself. **Roller-skating waitresses? Cool!**

"Hi," the waitress greeted George's family. "What can I get for you, folks?"

George knew exactly what he wanted. It was the same thing he always wanted when he was bummed out. "I'll have **a root beer float**," he said. "With **two scoops of chocolate ice cream**."

"I'll have vanilla ice cream with chocolate sauce," George's mother said.

"A double rocky road sundae for me," his dad added. **"With three cherries."**

"Okay, I'll get your order for you right away," the waitress promised.

As the waitress skated off, George began to feel a little better. **There was nothing a root beer float couldn't cure.**

And his parents didn't ask any more questions, either. His mom was talking about her store—ordering glass beads, needlepoint kits, and patterns for knitting afghans. George **didn't even know what an afghan was**. He didn't want to find out.

As his mom and dad talked, George sneaked another look inside Ernie's. Louie was sitting in a window booth with the three older boys. One of them looked a lot like Louie, only taller. Maybe it was his brother.

George couldn't hear what they were saying, but it was clear that it was funny because they were all laughing really, really hard. Just the way George's friends at his old school used to laugh whenever George said something funny. **Which was pretty much all the time.**

But that was the old George. The new George didn't joke around like that. Of course, the new George didn't have any friends, either.

"It's not fun not being funny," he whispered to himself.

Just then, the waitress skated over to George's table with the tray of ice cream. "Here you go," she said as she placed a huge mug of root beer and chocolate ice cream on the table. Then she passed his mom and dad their sundaes.

"Thanks," George said. "I really needed this."

He wrapped his lips around the straw and took a huge gulp of the fizzy, sweet root beer. "Yum!"

Just then, George's dad poked him. "Whoa!" he shouted. "Look up, son!"

George did, just in time to see a bright yellow star shoot across the night sky.

"It's a shooting star! Quick! Make a wish," his mom said. "And make it a good one because **wishes on shooting stars come true**."

George thought for a moment. "I want to make kids laugh but not get into trouble." he whispered. That wasn't such a big wish. It was the kind of wish that could come true, maybe.

George took another big gulp of his
root beer float. And then another. **He
couldn't drink that root beer fast
enough.**

He was slurping up the last bit of it
through a straw when, suddenly, George
began to hear strange gurgling noises
coming from the bottom of his belly. It
felt like there were hundreds of tiny
bubbles bouncing around in there.

The bubbles bounced up and down and all around. They ping-ponged their way from his belly to his chest, and bing-bonged their way up into his throat. And then . . .

B-U-U-U-R-P!

George let out a loud burp. He'd burped plenty of times before, but never one like this. The burp was so loud, it made the table shake. **It was so loud, his parents clapped their hands over their ears.**

The super burp was so loud that everyone sitting outside—and inside—Ernie's stopped talking and stared at George. **Then they started to laugh.** Hearing people laugh sounded just like the old days.

Then something else really strange happened. Suddenly George's hands reached across the table and grabbed two straws from the container.

It was like **his hands had a mind of their own**. George had no control over them. He watched as his hands shoved the straws up his nose. Then he jumped up on the table. It was like he was an **old-fashioned puppet** and someone had yanked him onto the table **by his strings**.

The next thing he knew, George's hands were clapping together, pretending they were flippers.

"Look, I'm a walrus," George shouted.

A bunch of kids shot up from their seats.

"Hey, check out that kid," one of them said. He was laughing, too.

"George, get down from there!" his mother and father both shouted.

But George couldn't get down. He couldn't stop himself. **Goofiness was just bubbling out of him.**

George do-si-doed and allemanded. His parents' sundaes went flying off the table.

"George!" his mother shouted. "You just got chocolate sauce all over my new blouse."

George stuck his **right foot in**. He stuck his **right foot out**. He did the hokey pokey and he turned himself about. And then . . .

Whoooosh. It felt like a giant bubble popped inside George's stomach. All the air rushed out of him. And so did the silliness. Suddenly George didn't feel so funny anymore. He stopped dancing and looked around.

"What are you doing up there?" his father asked.

"Um . . . the hokey pokey?" George answered. He didn't know what else to say. He wasn't sure why he'd jumped up on the table. He certainly hadn't planned it. It had just happened. Right after he'd let out that giant burp.

"I'm swearing off root beer floats for good," he promised himself. **"They're too dangerous."**

Chapter 6

George went up to his room as soon as he got home from the ice cream parlor. His parents looked puzzled. **He was puzzled, too.** Something had come over him—and that was **pretty freaky** to think about.

George sat down at his new desk in his new room. His homework assignment stared back at him.

Homework on his very first day at a new school. That just didn't seem fair. But there it was. And the right thing to do was work on it.

#1
GB

Following Directions
Your assignment tonight is to create something based on directions you find in a book or on the Internet. Tomorrow you will present your project to the class.

That didn't sound like a whole lot of fun. In fact it sounded kind of boring. **George leaned wa-a-ay back** in his chair until the two front legs were off the ground. It helped him to think better that way.

Maybe the assignment didn't have to be so boring. Maybe George could turn this following directions stuff into something he could have fun with.

There were three things George loved doing. One was **telling jokes**. Another was **skateboarding**. And the third was doing **magic tricks**.

George knew skateboarding was out of the question. That wouldn't be allowed in school. And there weren't really any directions for how to be a comedian. But a magic trick could work perfectly.

That was it! George would do a magic trick for his new class.

The kids would definitely think magic was cool to do. And Mrs. Kelly would be happy because you had to follow a lot of directions to get a magic trick just right.

George went over to his bookshelf and pulled out one of his magic books. Then he flipped the pages until he found **the perfect trick**. One he'd never done before.

After tomorrow, George wasn't going to be called the new kid anymore. He was going to be **the class magician**. Things were about to change—magically.

The next morning, George carried a small carton of eggs to school. The eggs were part of his magic trick. You were supposed to hard-boil them, but George hadn't had time last night to do that. So he just made sure to **hold the eggs really, really carefully**. George wanted to make sure that nothing went wrong. Today was going to be a good day. All that weird stuff last night at Ernie's was history. Forgotten.

Or maybe not . . . When he got to his classroom, the kid with the braces—Alex—dashed over to him.

He said, "Man, **is it true what you did at Ernie's last night**?"

George put the eggs on his desk and slipped off his backpack. "Well, I-I-I. Um. Sort of," he said slowly.

"Louie told me," Alex said.

"He's telling everyone."

Louie had seen him! George looked over at Louie's desk. Sure enough, he was whispering something to Mike and Max, and pointing at George.

"It was no big deal," George said.

Alex was about to say something else when Mrs. Kelly stood up in the front of the room. "Okay, everyone," she said. "Let's take our seats."

Phew. George was never so happy to have school start. Maybe by the time he'd done his trick, everyone would be talking about what a good magician he was, and not about last night at Ernie's. **George didn't want to be famous for being the kid with the big burp** who danced on tables with straws up his nose. That was the old George.

Chapter 7

"You cover the pinecone with peanut butter," Sage explained to the class in **her soft, high voice**. "And sprinkle birdseed all over. Then you hang the pinecone on a tree and watch the birds come to feed."

George **struggled hard not to yawn**. Making a birdfeeder thing wasn't very interesting. Neither was making a Popsicle stick box, or folding a piece of paper into a cat. So far no one had a presentation that was as cool as George's magic trick was going to be.

"Very nice, Sage," Mrs. Kelly said.

"It really works, too," Sage said. "I made one and put it in a pine tree. Birds come from all over the place to feed at it."

"That must be a wonderful sight to see." Then Mrs. Kelly said, "Who would like to go next?"

George raised his hand. So did Louie.

"Okay, Louie?" Mrs. Kelly said.

Louie walked to the front of the room.

He was carrying an electric guitar.

"I'm going to play a song I learned last night," Louie told the class. "I had to follow the directions in my songbook to learn the chords."

"What is your song called?" Mrs. Kelly asked.

"It's an old rock-and-roll song called '**Louie, Louie**,'" he answered. Then he plugged in the guitar and started to play.

George hated to admit it, but **Louie's presentation was pretty cool**.

When Louie finished the song, the whole class cheered. Max and Mike stuck their fingers in their mouths and **let out loud whistles**.

Louie smiled and took a bow.

"Great job, Louie," Mrs. Kelly said. "You're becoming quite a good guitarist."

As Louie walked back to his chair, Mrs. Kelly looked over at George. "Would you like to go next?" she asked.

George put on his magician's top hat, and **strode confidently to the front of the room**, holding his egg carton in his hands.

Louie sat at his desk with his arms folded across his chest. **He stared straight at George** with a look on his face that said, "I bet this is going to be really dumb."

Well, George was going to show him!

"I'm not George today," he told the

class. "I'm **the Great Georgini**! And I'm going to perform a magic trick that will astound and amaze you."

As he spoke, **George secretly dropped a mound of salt on Mrs. Kelly's desk**, making sure no one noticed what he was doing. He quickly covered the salt with a white cloth, just like the instructions had said to do.

Then he opened a small carton of six white eggs.

"Here are six ordinary eggs," the Great Georgini continued. "There's nothing magical about them. At least not until I use magic. **When I say the magic word, the eggs will stand up all by themselves!**"

George looked out at the class. Everyone was paying attention. Except for Louie, **they all seemed really into the trick**.

George placed an egg onto the white cloth and said, "Now everybody repeat after me—Abracadabra, zing, zang, zong!"

"Abracadabra, zing, zang, zong!" the class shouted back.

George slowly let go of the egg. "Tada!" he exclaimed.

Sure enough, the egg didn't roll over. It stood there on its own. Then George repeated with the other eggs. All six looked like they were standing up straight. They were really being held up by the pile of salt under the cloth, but the kids didn't know that.

"That's pretty awesome!" Julianna exclaimed.

"Not bad," Alex agreed.

"Magical," Sage added.

"How clever to do a magic trick. **Bravo, George**," Mrs. Kelly said with her big, gummy smile. "You have to follow directions perfectly to pull off a magic trick."

George smiled proudly. He was about to take his bow, when **suddenly he got a dizzy feeling in his head and a fizzy feeling in the pit of his stomach**. It felt like he'd just gulped down a huge root beer float—with a double scoop of chocolate ice cream.

Uh-oh.

The fizzy feeling was bing-bonging in his belly, and ping-ponging its way up into his chest. Just like it had the night before at the ice cream parlor.

Oh no! **What was happening?**

The kids were all staring at him. He opened his mouth. But all that came out was . . .

B-U-U-U-R-P!

Mrs. Kelly gasped. **This was no ordinary burp.** This was a supercolossal burp that blew papers off his teacher's desk. The kind of burp you could probably hear all the way from the moon!

Quickly, George started to cover his mouth. He wanted to say excuse me. But that's not what he did. **Not at all.**

Instead, George's hands began
acting up again. Just like last night!
They picked up the six eggs, and began
to juggle. That would have been really
cool—except for one thing. **George
had no idea how
to juggle.**

Crack. Splat. Yuck!

One by one, the eggs smashed onto the floor in **a gooey mess**. George frowned. Boy, it had really been a mistake not to hard-boil them the way the magic book said.

George knew that what he should do right now was clean up the mess as fast as possible. But his feet seemed to have other ideas. They wanted to **skid across the floor on the trail of egg slime**. So that was what George did . . . *wheee!* Then he turned around, opened his arms wide, and took a bow.

The kids were all clapping wildly. **But Mrs. Kelly wasn't.**

Whoosh. Suddenly George felt a huge bubble pop inside his stomach. All the air rushed right out of him. And so did all the silliness.

George wanted to say, "Whoops. I didn't mean to do that." So he opened his mouth and . . . those were exactly the words that came out of his mouth.

George looked at his teacher's face. **He had seen that look lots of times.** George was in big trouble, again.

Chapter 8

"I've heard about this boy," Mr. Coleman, the school janitor, said to Mrs. Kelly as he walked into the classroom with his mop and pail. "He's the one who caused that **ruckus** in the **cafeteria**."

George hadn't done anything wrong in the cafeteria. He'd just sneezed. But there was no point in arguing. **He was in enough trouble already.**

"Here," Mr. Coleman said to George. He shoved the mop into George's hands. "You made the mess. You clean up the mess."

"Yes, sir," he said. George began moving the wet mop over the gooey raw egg goop.

Swish. Swish. Swish. The sound of the moving mop was pretty much all George heard. It was very quiet in the room. The rest of the class had already gone to lunch. It was just George, Mr. Coleman, and Mrs. Kelly. **Two adults to one kid.**

"George, I understand that it's very hard to come into a new school, especially after the school year has started," Mrs. Kelly told him. "And I can tell you're a bright boy. But clowning around is not a good way to get to know everyone. **You need to try and use some self-control**."

George wanted to tell his teacher that he'd been trying really hard to control himself. The whole egg thing hadn't been in his control. After the burp, it was like something had just taken over him. But

how do you explain something like that to a teacher? Especially when George couldn't even explain it to himself.

Grumble. Rumble. George heard his stomach rumble. But he understood that he wasn't going to lunch until every drop of egg slime was cleaned up.

What George didn't understand was what had made him try to juggle the eggs. He hadn't planned on it. It wasn't part of the trick. It had just happened. He'd let out that giant burp, and then **everything went out of control**. Just like it had at Ernie's Ice Cream Emporium the night before.

George thought back to the night before. He'd seen the **shooting star**, made that wish about wanting to make kids laugh, and then along came the super burp and suddenly he was clowning around like crazy . . .

George smacked his forehead. That was it! **His wish had come true.** But it had also gone wrong . . . The part about not getting into trouble hadn't come true at all. **It was like that part of the wish had been cut off or something.**

George had wanted to be the one deciding when to fool around. But he wasn't. It was all up to the super burp!

That big, giant burp made him do stuff he didn't want to do. Goofy things. Bad stuff. Stuff that got George in trouble.

It was no ordinary burp. It was a magic super burp. **And it was ba-a-ad.**

George was really starving by the time the floor was cleaned up. He knew he had to hurry if he was going to get to the cafeteria in time for lunch.

There was only one problem. George couldn't remember where the cafeteria was. Julianna had taken him there yesterday because she was his buddy. But today he was on his own. And he was totally lost.

Then **George smelled something—** the familiar scent of spoiled milk, boiled hot dogs, and Jell-O. The smell of **school lunch**! All George had to do was follow his nose and he'd be in the cafeteria in no time.

Chapter 9

That afternoon after school, George hung out by himself. Again. But at least he had his skateboard—and his new **skateboard ramp**. His dad had built it for him near the loading dock behind his mom's store. The ramp led into an empty alleyway with no traffic. George could skate there as much as he wanted. **It was perfect.**

George tried to focus all of his attention on his skateboarding. He was good at controlling his moves on the board. A lot better than he was at

controlling the super burp, anyway. That thing had a mind of its own.

George pushed any thoughts of that stupid burp out of his head, and continued working on his ollie. The idea was to pop the skateboard up in the air and then land smoothly on the ground. George was determined to become **Grand Master of the Ollie**.

George stood at the top of his steep ramp. He pushed off, and then soared down the slope of the alleyway. Once he was going pretty fast, he put his back foot on the tail of his board and pushed down. At the same time, he slid his other foot forward. And then . . .

Wheee! George and the skateboard flew up into the air. It stayed there for a second. **George felt like he was flying.**

A moment later, the board landed on the ground, and George rolled down

the alleyway, with his legs crouched, his
arms spread for balance, and his mouth
smiling.

"Yes!" George exclaimed. He pumped
his fist into the air.

"Hey, that was cool!"

George turned around, surprised.

"You're pretty good," the kid said. He had short, blond hair and was wearing a T-shirt with a bolt of lightning on the front.

George stared at him. Pretty good? That had been a perfect ollie. A work of art.

"I'm also learning to do a 180-degree ollie," George told him. "The whole skateboard turns right around in midair."

"Cool," the kid said. "You looked like you were flashing across the sky. **Like a bolt of lightning**."

George smiled. "Thanks."

"Or the Green Lantern, or the Human Fly," the kid continued. **"I'm Chris**. I was on my way to the comic book store on the corner. I heard the noise back here."

"I'm George," George replied. **"I'm new here."**

"Yeah. I know."

George frowned. Had this kid already heard about the eggs-perience in the classroom? Or the table dancing at Ernie's? Or blowing snot on Louie's lunch?

But Chris didn't bring up any of those things. Instead, he just said, "I'm in Mrs. Miller's fourth-grade class."

"I have Mrs. Kelly," George said.

"So, how do you like the school?" Chris asked.

George shrugged. "I guess **Edith B. Boogerman Elementary School's** okay."

Chris laughed. "Boogerman. That's funny."

George looked at Chris strangely. He couldn't believe no one had ever called it that before. It was such an easy joke!

George smiled. This Chris kid seemed pretty nice. And he thought George was funny. Best of all, they went to the same school and were in the same grade. If Chris stuck around for a while longer, **this could officially count as hanging out with somebody**.

Chapter 10

Chris lived just a block away from George. So the next morning, George and Chris walked to school together.

Chris told George about a comic book he was writing. "I made up this superhero called **Toiletman**. His secret weapon is a toilet plunger. And he carries a roll of magic toilet paper to tie up the bad guys."

"Sounds good," George said.

Then he smiled. "Do you know what one toilet said to the other toilet?"

"What?" Chris asked.

"You look a little flushed." George laughed at his own joke.

Chris laughed, too. "Hey, can I use that in my comic book?"

"Sure," George said. "**Maybe I can help with your comic**. I know lots of jokes."

The boys had just reached the schoolyard when they saw Alex.

George waved to him. Then he flipped up his skateboard with one foot and grabbed it with his hand.

George was proud of his board. It was red and black with **a really spooky painting of a bat skeleton** in the middle.

"That's the coolest board I've ever seen," Alex said.

"Thanks," George said. "You can try it if you want."

"I've seen him on his skateboard," Chris told Alex. "He's amazing."

George smiled.

Just then, Louie walked over. "You guys want to play **killer ball** before school?" he asked Chris and Alex.

Alex shook his head. "Later maybe," he told Louie. **"I want to try out George's skateboard."**

"I bet you can't even ride that thing," Louie said to George.

George just smiled. He didn't have to prove he could skateboard. **He knew he could.**

Just then the bell rang. It was time to go inside.

"Saved by the bell, huh, New Kid?" Louie said.

George pretended not to hear Louie. He picked up his skateboard and walked into the school building.

I'll show you, George thought to himself.

Just not right this minute.

Chapter 11

"We have gym class after this," Alex whispered to George as the class worked on their math sheets that morning. **"I hope Mr. Trainer's back."**

"Me too," George whispered. Otherwise he'd have to do-si-do and promenade again. That hadn't gone so well the first time.

They both stopped talking and went back to their math sheets because Mrs. Kelly was going around the room checking the kids' work. **She was only one row away.**

Suddenly, George felt a little bubble inside—kind of like he was going to burp.

"Here comes **Mrs. Smelly**," he said.

Oops. The words had just popped out of his mouth. He hadn't meant to say them. Although the name fit. Mrs. Kelly's perfume was really smelly.

Now the bubbles started to ping-pong around. All on their own. George's eyes crossed and his tongue hung out.

"That perfume is gonna make me pass out."

Oh no! Those words had come out all on their own, too. And the bubbles were getting stronger.

George held his breath, trying to force the burp down. But Alex had heard everything and was laughing. Mrs. Kelly seemed to know it was George who had made Alex laugh.

Please, not now. No magic burp, George thought to himself.

"Alex! George!" Mrs. Kelly scolded. She was not smiling her gummy smile now. "**I had no idea double-digit multiplication was that funny.** Do you want to share the joke with the rest of the class?"

Alex stopped laughing really fast. "No," he told her. "Sorry."

George just kept holding his breath. He shook his head, but didn't open his mouth. Then, a second later, he felt as if a bubble gum bubble went *pop!* inside him. Yessss! **George had squelched the belch!**

In the gym, a huge black-and-white soccer ball came rolling toward George. It was just like a regular soccer ball, only huge. **Like a soccer ball for giants.** It was the biggest ball George had ever seen.

A tall, skinny man with dark brown hair and a moustache was behind the rolling ball. He was wearing shorts and had a whistle around his neck. George figured he had to be Mr. Trainer, the gym teacher.

"We're playing **crab soccer**," Julianna explained. "It's just like regular soccer, except you sit down while you're playing."

Julianna sat down with her feet flat on the floor. She placed her hands on the floor with her fingers facing outward. Then she lifted her body and began to walk on her hands and feet.

George laughed. **She did sort of look like a crab.**

"Now you try it," Julianna urged George.

George tried to copy what Julianna was doing. But **it wasn't so easy moving his hands and feet at the same time**. He wasn't going nearly as fast as Julianna was.

"Our team is trying to get the ball in the goal over there," Julianna said. She

pointed across the gym.

Mr. Trainer blew his whistle. The kids all began crab crawling around the floor.

Alex kicked the ball really hard. It was headed right for the goal. But Louie was a quick crab. He blocked the ball, and kicked it back toward the other side of the gym.

"Go Louie!" Max shouted.

"Nice save!" Mike cheered.

George scrambled to get in front of the ball so he could kick it away. But **then it happened**. **Again.** Something started to bubble up in George's belly. It was stronger than it had been in math class.

The bubbles were already ping-ponging around in his stomach and threatening to move up into his chest. He'd done it once before. Now he had to do it again. **He had to beat the burp!**

Quickly, George shut his lips tight, trying to lock the bubbles in and then he flipped over and did a handstand against the wall. The bubbles were still trying to escape. But now George was upside down. If the

bubbles moved up, they'd go into his feet. There was no way out from there!

"Young man!" Mr. Trainer cried out. "What are you doing?"

George didn't know what to say. He couldn't exactly tell his gym teacher that he was trying to squelch a belch!

"George! Watch out!" Julianna shouted suddenly.

Upside down, George saw the huge soccer ball careening across the gym floor.

It was coming straight at George's head!

Quickly, George flipped over. He landed on his rear end and then kicked the oncoming ball as hard as he could.

Bam! The giant crab soccer ball went soaring across the room.

"Goal!" Mr. Trainer shouted.

"Awesome kick!" Julianna said.

Out of the corner of his eye, George could see Louie. **He looked really mad.** George had a feeling he was the one who had kicked the ball right at his head.

But that didn't really matter to George. Neither did how far he'd kicked the giant crab soccer ball. Or that **his team was ahead**.

George was just happy he'd won out over the super burp.

At least for now.

Chapter 12

At lunch, George sat with Chris, Alex, and Julianna. They were pretty nice kids. And not once, for the rest of the day, did George feel even one bubble in his belly. All through recess and art class he felt **100 percent like an ordinary kid**.

Art class had been especially fun because the kids were starting to make their papier-mâché piñatas. George loved sloshing around in the **soupy, goopy, papier-mâché paste** as he built his piñata.

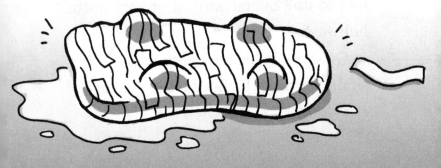

In fact, he was having so much fun that he didn't even get mad when Mike told him his skateboard piñata looked like a big, white tongue. Which it absolutely did not.

George was actually feeling pretty good about things when the bell for dismissal rang. And then he heard Louie calling him.

"Hey, New Kid. Are you ready to show us what a hot skateboarder you are?"

Louie was mocking George. **But so what?**

"Sure. Meet me outside," George told Louie.

"Yeah right," Louie said. "You'll probably sneak out the back entrance."

Mike and Max laughed.

George frowned. **What did Louie expect him to do?** Skateboard right here in the hallway?

George put his backpack and his skateboard on the floor. Then he started to put on his helmet so he would be ready to skate as soon as he got outside. As he was buckling his helmet strap under his chin, George got a strange feeling in his stomach. A bunch of bubbles were suddenly bouncing up and down and all around in his belly.

Oh no! Not again!

George tried desperately to stop the bubbles. He held his nose and clamped his mouth shut. But the bubbles were strong. He'd kept them down before, but George wasn't sure he could do it again.

"George, what's wrong?" Alex asked. **"Your face is turning purple."**

The bubbles ping-pong-pinged their way up out of George's stomach.

They boing-bing-boinged their way to his chest.

They bing-boing-binged their way up his throat. And then . . .

George let out the **loudest burp** in the **history of Edith B. Sugarman Elementary School**. In fact, it was possibly the loudest burp ever burped in the history of all elementary schools. A super-duper mega burp! The burps at the ice cream shop and in his classroom were **baby burps** compared to this one.

Suddenly all the talking in the hallway stopped. Everyone turned to stare at George.

"It wasn't me!" George declared.

But **there was no hiding it**. George was the big burper. Everyone had heard it. Now everyone was laughing.

And then suddenly, George's feet wanted to jump on his skateboard right here in the middle of the school. George tried to stop them by grabbing onto Alex's shoulder.

"Are you okay?" Alex asked.

George couldn't stop himself. The super burp had taken over. He tried to keep holding onto Alex. But all at once his hands let go. They weren't cooperating.

And neither were his feet. They leaped onto the board. And before he knew what was happening, **George was rolling down the halls**.

He shifted his weight to the back of the board and . . . *wheee!* He took off into the air and turned the board around in a circle. **A perfect 180!**

"Satisfied?" George shouted as he passed by Louie.

"George!" Mrs. Kelly came racing out of the classroom. "Get off that skateboard right now!"

But George didn't get off. He couldn't. **It was like his feet were cemented to the board.**

"Woo-hoo!" George shouted as he popped up into the air in another ollie.

Kids started clapping and whistling.

"Check this out!" George called to the kids. He turned the corner ready to do an awesome **pop shove-it**.

George looked over his shoulder. He could see Mr. Trainer running after him.

"I'll put a stop to this!" Mr. Trainer shouted to Mrs. Kelly. But George was too fast for him.

Practically every kid at Edith B. Sugarman Elementary School was trailing after **George and his runaway skateboard**. George jumped up and landed back down on the skateboard.

As he passed her office, the principal came running out into the hall. "George

Brown! There is no skateboarding allowed in school!" she shouted as he whizzed by.

George knew that. The principal didn't understand. The burp was in control, not George. He turned his head and tried to say, "I'm sorry." But nothing came out.

"George! **Watch out**!" someone shouted. George thought it sounded like Alex.

When George turned back around, he saw what the problem was. He was **heading straight for the art room** at the end of the hallway. The door was open. George was going too fast to stop. Besides, the magic burp wouldn't let him.

"Whoa!" he shouted as he whizzed into the room and smashed into a table.

Ride over.

Whoosh. Suddenly George felt a big

bubble pop right in the middle of his stomach. The air just rushed right out of him.

The super burp had disappeared. But George was still here, left to deal with the mess.

He fell off his skateboard and landed on his rear end just as a pail of **icky,**

sticky, papier-mâché goo tipped over.
Yucky, white papier-mâché rained down
over George's head.

George sat there, feeling the slippery,
ooey-gooey, white paste **slither down his
neck**, and ooze down under his shirt. It
dripped on George's face and into his
mouth. Blech. It was the most disgusting

thing George had ever tasted. And considering he'd once mixed **tuna fish with chocolate ice cream and ketchup**, that was saying a lot.

"Hey, check it out," Alex said. "George is a human piñata."

The kids were all crowding in the doorway.

"Nice job, New Kid," Louie said in a mean voice.

George sighed. New Kid. **There were those two words again.**

"You're in some mess now," Louie told George.

George sat there for a minute, staring up at Louie. He didn't say a word. What could he say? **Louie was right.**

"George!" Mrs. Kelly exclaimed as she ran into the art room. "Why would you do that? Just what got into you?"

George sighed. It was actually what

had gotten out of him that had made him act all goofy. But **what was he supposed to say**? The burp made me do it? That would just get him into more trouble.

More trouble was the last thing George needed.

Chapter 13

That afternoon, George walked home alone—again. He'd had to stay after school to clean up the art room. That had taken a really long time since the principal wouldn't let Chris or Alex stay to help. By the time he'd finished, all the kids had gone home.

Well, **one thing was for sure**. No one was going to call George the new kid anymore. **Everyone knew his name**— including the art teacher, the janitor, and the school principal, Mrs. McKeon. He'd spent a lot of time talking to her before she let him go home.

George reached up and scratched at his head. The papier-mâché paste was starting to harden in his hair. **It was all clumped behind his ears, too.** He was going to have to take a really long shower tonight. **Then he'd have to clean up the dirty tub.**

And after that, his parents would talk about being responsible. George could just hear his mother asking, "What happened to the new George?"

Worst of all, his parents would probably take away his skateboard for a week or two.

Why me? George thought as he walked through Beaver Brook on his way home. Of all the millions of kids on the planet, why am I the one to get stuck with this stupid, magic super burp? It didn't seem fair.

George had a feeling **he hadn't seen the last of the burp**. It was going to come back. But who knew when? All George knew for sure was that he would have to work hard to stop it when it did. Because if he let that burp out, there was no telling what might happen next!

About the Author

Nancy Krulik is the author of more than 150 books for children and young adults including three *New York Times* best sellers and the popular Katie Kazoo, Switcheroo books. She lives in New York City with her family, and many of George Brown's escapades are based on things her own kids have done. (No one delivers a good burp quite like Nancy's son, Ian!) Nancy's favorite thing to do is laugh, which comes in pretty handy when you're trying to write funny books!

About the Illustrator

Aaron Blecha was raised by a school of giant squid in Wisconsin and now lives with his wife in London, England. He works as an artist and animator designing toys, making cartoons, and illustrating books, including the Zombiekins series. You can enjoy more of his weird creations at www.monstersquid.com.